4/80

TOM FOBBLE'S DAY

TOM FOBBLE'S DAY

ALAN GARNER

Etchings by Michael Foreman

COLLINS

First United States edition published in 1979
by William Collins Publishers, Inc., New York
and Cleveland.

Text copyright © 1977 by Alan Garner
Illustrations copyright © 1977 by Michael Foreman

Originally published in 1977 by
William Collins Sons & Co., Ltd., London
and Glasgow. All rights reserved. Printed
in the United States of America.

Library of Congress Cataloging in Publication Data

Garner, Alan.
    Tom Fobble's day.

SUMMARY: When his sled is "Tom Fobbled" by another
boy, William's grandfather makes him another from an
old oak loom.
    [1. England—Fiction] I. Foreman, Michael,
1938- II. Title.
PZ7.G18417To 1979 [Fic] 78-26927
ISBN 0-529-05507-4

FOREWORD

Tom Fobble's Day is one of a quartet of books by Alan
Garner. The other titles are *The Stone Book, Granny
Reardun,* and *The Aimer Gate.* Each book stands on its
own, but together they form a saga tracing four
generations of a working class family in Chorley, a
small town in Cheshire, England.

In *The Stone Book* we meet Mary and her
stonemason father; Mary's son is Joseph, the "granny
reardun" of the second book; Robert, the boy who
thinks he might become a soldier like his Uncle
Charlie in *The Aimer Gate,* is Joseph's son; and
William, whose sled is "Tom Fobbled" in the final
book, is Joseph's grandson. The first book is set in
Victorian England; the last takes place during World
War II.

5

Alan Garner grew up in the area of England in which the quartet is set, and he has a deep familiarity with the people of whom he writes. The simplicity of his style in these books is meticulous, poetic—and perfectly suited to their universal and deeply moving themes. For beneath the surface of the stories, which are engrossing in themselves, the author probes the mysteries of his characters' linkage with their ancestors and with the deeper past. They search for their individual identities; they meet danger with courage; they mitigate poverty with humor; they experience love and joy; and they face with stoicism the inevitability of death. The books, though brief and unpretentious, have an elemental universality rather like Greek plays, which indeed have been very much a part of Alan Garner's literary background.

The language he has chosen to use is a combination of modern English with the old northwest Mercian spoken pattern. Many words from the past are still in everyday use in rural Cheshire, and Garner uses them without apology or explanation in the books. This may give some readers pause, but their use is so natural that their meaning is obvious, and they deepen and enrich both the credibility and the power of the books.

for Joseph

TOM FOBBLE'S DAY

"Tom Fobble's Day!"

The first snowball caught William in the teeth. The second burst on his forehead; the third on his balaclava helmet.

He let go of his sledge, and ran, blindly. The snowballs kept hitting him, on the back, on the legs, softly, quietly, but he couldn't stand them.

The snow gathered between the iron of his clogs and the curved wood of the sole and built into rockers of ice. His ankles twisted, and he fell over, trying not to cry. He curled himself against the attack.

But it had stopped. He opened his eyes. He wasn't even out of range. Stewart Allman had stopped throwing and was sitting on William's sledge.

William stood up. "Give us me sledge!" It had taken him a day and a morning to build it out of an old crate.

"It isn't yours," said Stewart Allman.

"It is!"

"It isn't. I've Tom-Fobbled it."

"You can't! You can't Tom-Fobble sledges! Only marbles!"

"What are you going to do about it?" said Stewart Allman.

"And only after Easter!" William was getting more angry than he was scared.

"It is after Easter," said Stewart Allman. "Last Easter!" He laughed.

William charged. The snow on his clogs made him trip, and he rolled down the hill and Stewart Allman sat on him.

"Easter! Tom Fobble's Day's Easter and marbles! You know it is!"

Stewart Allman pushed a handful of snow into William's mouth.

"I only want to lend it, you boiled ha'penny," he said. "We'll take it in turns."

"Where's yours?" said William.

"Bust," said Stewart Allman.

Lizzie Leah's was the place where everybody went to sledge. It was two fields, one above the other and above the road. The bottom field was short and steep, and all that had to be done was to stop before the thorn hedge. The top field was long, and there was a gate in the corner to the bottom field. But there weren't many who could sledge the top field, corner to corner, across the slope, and through the gate and down the bottom field.

It was fast, and the sledge had to be turned sharply for the gate, and at the only patch in the whole field where it could be turned, there was a hump that made the sledge take off. And the chances for the sledge then were to land against a tree, or in barbed wire, or the gatepost, or to go through to the bottom field.

"I'll swap you," said William.

"What for?" said Stewart Allman.

"An incendiary," said William.

"Show us."

William pulled the incendiary bomb out of his jacket inside pocket. He had found it that morning, after the air raid. The bomb was the shape of a bicycle pump, but corroded and sticky, like an old battery.

"OK," said Stewart Allman. "I'll swap."

He pulled both his trouser pockets out, and two piles of shrapnel dropped into the snow. "Hot last night," he said. Shrapnel picked up hot from the gunfire was worth more than cold-found. "Give us the sledge."

"I meant swap you instead of lending," said William.

"I didn't," said Stewart Allman.

"You'll bust it," said William.

"You have first go, then," said Stewart Allman.

William collected up the shrapnel. It was a jagged, brown metal, sharp enough to cut and to pierce, and even its surface was harsh, like sand.

"All right," he said. He put the shrapnel in his jacket, and walked along the bottom field to where the girls had a sledge run.

"Top field," said Stewart Allman.

Stewart Allman's sledge had been wrecked against the tree. William went a few yards above the hump and turned his sledge round.

"Is that all you're doing?" said Stewart Allman.

"It's new," said William. He lay down on the sledge. It was no longer than his chest, and his head stuck out.

"Want a shove?" said Stewart Allman.

William got up and sat on the sledge, holding the string.

"You're frit," said Stewart Allman.

"Don't care," said William. He pushed with his feet. The sledge moved and sank into the snow and stopped. He tried again, and slipped forward off the front of the sledge. The third time, the thin, flat runners passed over the ridge of snow they had built, and William was away.

He wasn't going fast enough at the hump, and had to heel himself along to get over. He rode down the bottom field and braked before he reached the hedge.

"How is it?" Stewart Allman shouted.

"Smashing!"

William pulled the sledge back up the hill. Stewart Allman had climbed to the middle of the top field and was waiting. The middle of the top field was as high as it was safe for the best sledgers to go. William had to stop to knock the snow off his clogs.

"Don't be all day," said Stewart Allman.

"You've got boots," said William.

"What's that sissy way of riding?" said Stewart Allman.

"It's my sledge," said William.

"You look a right betty."

Stewart Allman lay on the sledge and bent his knees. "Shove us," he said.

William took hold of Stewart Allman's feet and ran as if he was pushing a cart.

"Let go!"

William fell over.

The rickety crate bobbed down the field. William thought it would shake to pieces, but it didn't. He saw it hit the hump and turn in the air. Stewart Allman had his foot down hard just before he left the ground. He was through the gate and out of sight behind the hedge between the fields.

William waited. He heard a cry.

"You what?" he shouted.

He heard the cry again, but couldn't tell what Stewart Allman was saying.

He set off down the field, following the tracks. They turned at the hump, and there was a gap before they began again.

The brow of the bottom field hid the road hedge. If there had been an accident, there was no one else on Lizzie Leah's to help him.

But Stewart Allman was sitting by the hedge. He had pulled up exactly right. The marks of his toecaps had dug down to the frozen grass to brake him. The lines of green looked wrong in the snow.

"What's up?" said William.

"Nowt," said Stewart Allman. "It's your turn."

"Why couldn't you bring it back?" said William.

"It's not mine," said Stewart Allman.

"You should've fetched it!"

Stewart Allman began to make snowballs.

William took his turn from the same place as before, but kicked harder and had enough speed to ride the hump. At the bottom he waited for Stewart Allman, but he didn't come, so William went back up the field.

"One more," said William, "then I'm off."

"What doing?"

"I must go see me Grandad."

"Why now?"

"I must catch him while he's at work. And anyroad, it's going to snow a blizzard."

"You can't tell that," said Stewart Allman. "Sun's shining."

"It isn't at the back of Saint Philip's," said William.

The sky was clear, but behind the church and across the plain there was a cloud that made the seagulls white against it, and the weathercock on the church was golden.

"Snow's not that color," said Stewart Allman. "Snow's not black. You're daft."

"It's still last goes," said William.

"I tell you what," said Stewart Allman. "You lie on top of me, and I'll steer, and we'll get a fair old baz up with that weight."

"No," said William.

18

"Are you frit again?"

"It'd squash your gas mask."

"Mardy!" said Stewart Allman, and ran down the hill, pushing the sledge in front of him. When he could run no faster, he dived on and was away.

As he reached top speed, just before the hump, the left-hand runner began to squirm. Even William could see the movement. Stewart Allman tried to brake, but couldn't, and he lost direction by putting both toes down. The runner cracked, and the sledge lifted into the air sideways, and Stewart Allman rolled with it so that the sledge was between him and the gatepost. William heard the crunch and the smash and was already running. The shrapnel chimed in his pockets.

"I've bent me incendiary," said Stewart Allman. "Whatever made you think that was a sledge?" He held the splintered boxwood dangling together on lengths of tin. "Two in one day's not bad, is it? Shall you be coming after tea?"

"How can I, now you've bust me sledge?" said William.

"Oh, there'll be plenty tonight," said Stewart Allman, "never fret. And it's a bomber's moon—should be good."

"I'll have to see," said William.

"Play again, then?" said Stewart Allman.

"Play again," said William.

William left his sledge on the pile of other broken sledges and set off for the village.

Grandad's house was at the bottom of Lizzie Leah's, and it was a measured mile from the house to where he worked. William tried to pace it, one thousand seven hundred and sixty strides, but his stride wasn't a yard long and the snow packed under his clogs, and the wind came with the blizzard out of the cloud.

The worst part of sledging was always after. The flakes melted in his balaclava, and he had to keep sucking the chinpiece

20

to keep it from rubbing sore. His mouth tasted of sweet wool. He drew his hands up inside his jacket sleeves, but his khaki mittens were wet. His trousers chafed below his knees, and his sock garters were tight. Each kneecap was blue.

The air-raid siren sounded the alert. The alert often went during the day, although the bombers came only at night.

William crossed the village street in frog hops and giant strides to reach the grid above the ironmonger's cellar where Grandad worked. He made it: one thousand seven hundred and sixty yards, jumps and strides.

William stood on the grid. He could see Grandad's bench below, and the silver gleam of his hair.

William sniffed the drop off his nose. He was cold. He dragged his feet sideways across the grating, to free his clogs, but all he did was to push loose snow onto Grandad's window.

"Oh, flipping heck," said William.

He had been watching the silver of Grandad's hair: now he was looking at his blue eyes and sharp red nose.

He went into the empty shop. The bell tinkled on its curled spring.

At the back of the shop there was a yard door that slid in grooves. William could open it with one finger, because Grandad had made a lead counterweight and hung it by a sash cord, so that the door was balanced. Behind the big green door was the farrier's yard, where horses used to be shod, and from the yard broad steps went down to Grandad's cellar and forge and the flat, square cobbles.

It was forever dark at the forge. Light came from the grating and made silhouettes of all the heavy gear: the hoists, the tackle, the presses, the anvils, and the skirt of the forge hood.

Coals burned dull red. Under the grating was the bench where Grandad sat. He

was the whitesmith and locksmith, and blacksmith, too.

His crucible stood in a firebrick bed, full of solder. His irons were by him, some so big that lifting them made William's wrists ache. But he had seen Grandad take them, and heat them, and when they were hot, Grandad spat on them; and the spit danced, and he ran his thumb along the end to test the heat.

And then he took metal and did wonderful things: turning, twisting, tapping, shaping, dabbing and making, quickly before the metals were cold. Brew cans, billy cans, milk cans, and the great churns that stood at the roadside. He could make them all. And he could make brass fenders straight, and take the dents from tin, and put back the fragile lion masks on coal scuttles.

"I've a month's mind to tan your hide," said Grandad. "What were you standing out there for, fair starved, and the siren blahting?"

"It's a false alarm," said William. "Or snow got into it."

"And what if somebody doesn't tell Gerry one of these days, and he finds you gawping up at him?" said Grandad.

"That's what I've come for," said William. "We have to have our names written in indelible on all our clothes, and Mum says can you stamp mine on me clogs, please?"

Grandad put his tools down and looked at William. William swung his gas-mask tin off his shoulder and sat on it.

"And what's the indelible in aid of?" said Grandad.

"We were told in prayers. We've to be ready for inspection on Monday, or else."

"I see," said Grandad. "And what are you doing clagged up so you can't hardly walk?"

"I keep stopping to scrawk it off," said William.

"Come here," said Grandad. "I don't

25

know. What do they learn you these days?"

William leant against the bench, and Grandad put a clog between his knees, with his back to William, as if he was shoeing a horse, and knocked the snow off with a hammer.

"Hold still," he said, and he reached over to where his metal punches stood in their rack in order of the alphabet, and very deftly he took each as he needed it, placed the letter against the sole of William's clog and tapped it. The punch left a clean print in the wood. And he dropped the punch back in the rack, and took another.

Grandad finished William's name on one clog, and swapped legs.

"I reckon," said Grandad, "that in fifty-five years of setting labels on milk cans for farmers, I must've come near writing a book with these. And now I'm stamping you up so as we can go looking for what's left of you next time you gawp at bombers. I don't know. I really do not know. Hold still, will you?"

He dipped a worn paintbrush into a tin and daubed something stiff and smooth over the soles of William's clogs. "There," he said, "that'll keep the snow off. But mind how you treat your Mother's rugs, or she'll play the dickens with the both of us."

"What is it?" said William.

"Axle grease."

William sat down by the forge again. "Can you do anything for the leathers?" he said. "They're that stiff all the time, I have to warm them to take them off. They're crippling me."

"Worse could happen," said Grandad. "Bad shoes have saved my life."

"How?" said William.

"In Kaiser Bill's War," said Grandad. "I went for me medical, along with all the other youths from this shop—Tommy Latham, David Peters, and them. But the army doctor said as how he reckoned they could manage without me. He said, 'You've hammer toes.' And I said, 'What do you expect? I'm a smith!' But it was a terrible rough auction, was Kaiser Bill's War. Men were going thick and threefold. Like water down a ditch.

"They're all on the Memorial at Saint Philip's. George Powell, Oliver Leah, the Burgesses; Fred, Jim, Percy, Reg. And me own half brother, Charlie. He's there. And he was the one me Mother reared. For that."

The forge was low, but warm enough to chill William's clothes with melting.

The all clear sounded. William and Grandad looked through the window, crisscrossed with strips of brown paper against blast. The blizzard had stopped.

"I brought these down from up home this morning," said Grandad.

He went to a row of vises clamped to a bench. In the vises were two strips of iron, about six feet long, and beveled on one side. Grandad had drilled holes in each strip and countersunk them.

"Get on the bellows, youth," he said.

William began to work the lever handle of the forge bellows up and down. It was as though the cellar was waking, breathing. The coals glowed more brightly, and blue gases licked around them.

Up and down, up and down. The warmth came back.

"Steady," said Grandad. "We're not the Queen Elizabeth, nor Chapel organ, neither. Steady. Keep her going gentle."

He held an end of one of the strips in the forge. When the end was cherry red, he lifted it over to his swage block.

In all Grandad's forge and cellar there was nothing like the swage block. It was a square, thick slab, too heavy for William even to move, but Grandad could move it. Its edges were indented, but each indentation was a different size, a different shape. They were slots, for bevels or angles. And the block itself was pierced by squares and circles, so that the weight looked light, and in one corner was a hollow, a circular dish when the block lay that way.

It was a shape older than anvils.

Yet it was only a block of iron, to be used any side up, for anything that was useful.

Grandad put the hot end into a hole in the swage block, and pulled down until the strip began to bend. He drew it out a short way, and bent it again. The metal was losing its color.

"Now," said Grandad. "Give her a good un! Come on! Queen Elizabeth, Chapel, and all!"

The lever went up and down, and William with it. The forge roared. Grandad held the strip with long pincers and paddled it in the fire. He kept looking at the bellows handle, as if he was measuring it, but most of the time he was watching the heated iron.

"You'll often wonder why a smith works in the dark," he said, "and here's why. It's

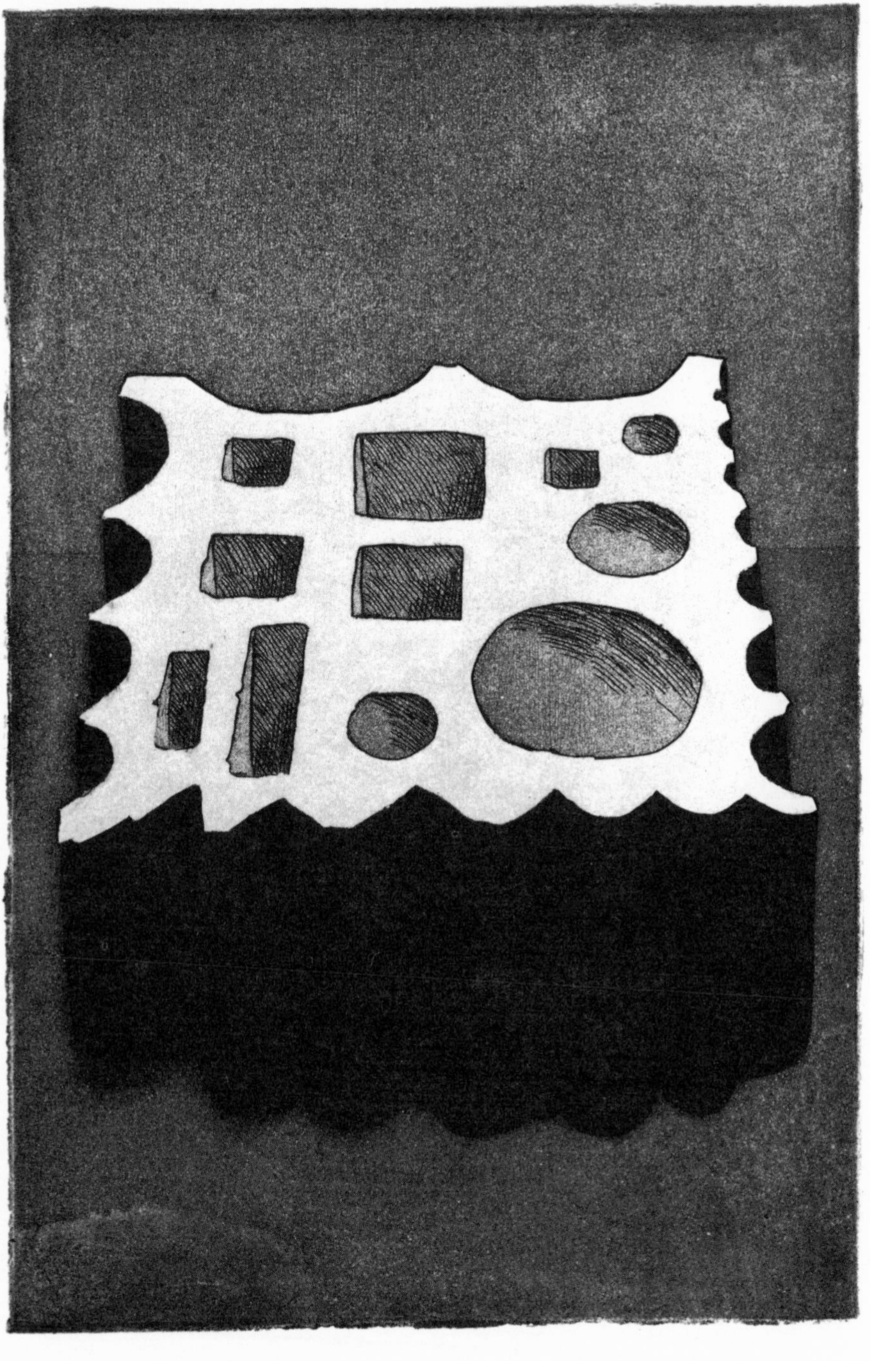

nothing dubious. You can't judge color if the sun's putting your fire out. It's pale straw we're after: pale straw, and not a touch lighter. See!"

He pulled out the strip. Where he had bent it in the swage block was yellow but not white. He moved quickly now and turned the rough bend in the hollow cup, pressing but not forcing the softened iron to the perfect curve, so that the cup in the block gave its shape to his hand. Then he laid the strip aside. It changed from straw to cherry.

"We'll not need to quench it," he said.

Grandad took the second strip and did the same to that as he had done to the first, until the two were side by side, identical.

"Leave her now," he said to William. "She'll do."

The fire receded. Grandad flicked the swage block clean with the end of his leather brat, and wiped his face. He sat with William by the forge and drew two cups of beer from the barrel he kept under his bench.

William drank, and watched.

"I'll tell you something," said Grandad. "When I was a young youth, and wed, we had the Boer War. And I was playing E-flat cornet for the Temperance Band. And every time we killed two Boers we had us a carnival. Well, there came this night when we'd killed three, and didn't we celebrate! Charlie and me, we were that fresh we had to play leaning against the wall. And Ollie Leah was sat on the floor there, out in the middle of the road. He played the big drum, and they said as he was the only one to keep time sat down. I suppose there's a Memorial to them Boers somewhere, if we only knew. But there was no wireless, you see.

"Now in Kaiser Bill's War we were working all hours on horseshoes. And that was on top of the regular jobs. I shifted fifteen ton of shoe iron myself. And fifteen ton is thirty-three thousand six hundred shoes. Eight thousand four hundred horses. It took us all our time."

Grandad threw the last drops of beer into the fire, and wiped his moustache. He bounced the two strips against the palm of his hand. They were cool. He pulled the bellows handle down and laid each strip along the wood. The iron was a perfect fit, lying close, and curving with the end.

Grandad pushed the handle up once and pulled it down again. The bellows breathed and the fire brightened. Grandad stood up and unbolted the handle. He took the long wood to the bench, laid it carefully, and bent to examine the grain. Then he took a chisel and held it to the wood, and he hit the chisel with a hammer. There was a sound like muslin tearing, and the handle ripped, split apart down its length, clean as if a saw had done it.

"That's a good bit of ash," said Grandad. "I thought it was, the first day I set eyes on it."

"But what are you doing?" said William.

"Doing? I've done."

Grandad and William stood in the cellar. Light was going from window and fire.

"Fifty-five years," said Grandad. "I reckon it's best left now. Did you not know it was me last day?"

William shook his head.

"Come on," said Grandad. "We've a job to finish."

He went to his bench. His irons and punches were ready for work. Everywhere was clean in the dirt. He untied his brat from round his waist, used it to flick the anvils, the vises, the bench, and the swage block of dust, and hung it on a nail. His hand touched everything once.

"She'll do," said Grandad.

Grandad and William went out of the cellar up the steps to the farrier's yard. Grandad's bicycle was in the yard. He tied the iron and the split handle onto the frame, put on his cap and his trouser clips, wheeled the bicycle into the street, and locked the door.

"There," he said. He gave William the key. It was so worn that the teeth were smooth, the whole key thin from wearing out pockets.

"It was me first prentice piece. I cut a new one just before the sirens went. That's a lifetime for you."

William held the key. It was metal like a pebble from the brook. Every part was soft and rounded, without edges. He wrapped it in his handkerchief, so that the shrapnel wouldn't scratch it.

Grandad switched on his front and rear lamps, and mounted the bicycle.

"Jump up," he said, "and we'll go home and make ourselves some tea."

William sat on the carrier over the back mudguard. He had one arm around Grandad and the other over the bellows handle.

Grandad pushed off and began his ride home. He always went at the same pace, steadily, ignoring hills.

"Hold still," he said, "else you'll have us in the ditch."

But it was hard. The carrier was sharp, the wind cold, and there was nowhere for William's feet. He had to let them hang wide of the wheel. The tires swished on the packed snow. His face was in Grandad's coat, and he could feel the movement of pedaling through the heavy folds. The leather saddle squeaked, and its springs copied the road.

"Near enough," said Grandad, "with it being a measured mile, and allowing four trips a day until I lost your Grandma, and two a day since, what with not coming home for dinner, I calculate I've biked this road for work equivalent to two and a half times round the world at the equator."

It was night when they reached home, but the snow reflected the rising moon on the thatch and the whitewashed walls.

Grandad put his bicycle in the coal shed and shoveled a bucket of coal to last the evening. They went into the house and hung the blackout curtains over the windows before they lit the lamps. Grandad poked the fire. He had banked it up with slack before going to work, and the coal dust was glowing under the dead surface.

"I'll put the kettle on and wash me," said Grandad, "while you go and fetch some spuds in."

William took a basket from the kitchen and went to the garden.

The potatoes had been hogged for the winter. The hogg was a shallow pit, big as a room, and the potatoes were stacked in it, pitched like a roof to throw the rain off, covered with soil and bracken to keep out the cold.

William pulled the bracken away from the hogg where it had been opened, filled the basket, and covered the hogg again.

When he was back inside the house he took off his balaclava and mittens and put them on the fender to dry.

Grandad was washing his hands in a tin basin. William turned on the tap over the slopstone. "Get the muck off and leave the jackets," said Grandad. "We'll have them in the oven."

William tugged the earth away in frozen lumps. "There's a yard of frost out there," he said. "Grandad?"

"Ay?"

"What if somebody shouts Tom Fobble's Day on you, and it's not for marbles and you're not after Easter?"

"Is he bigger than you?" said Grandad.

"Yes."

"Then run like beggary."

"It's Stewart Allman," said William. "He took me sledge and wrecked it."

"And good riddance," said Grandad. "I never saw such a codge."

Grandad wiped his hands on the harsh towel. William held the potatoes under the tap. A ball of earth came away solid. He broke it open in his hands.

"Eh up!" said Grandad.

The earth was like a split rock. In the middle of the black ball, clean, white, shining, was a clay pipe. The pipe was decorated in fluted lines, and was undamaged.

William laid the earth gently on the slopstone and let the water trickle from the tap. He took a piece of shrapnel out of his pocket and used its jagged point to help the earth loose.

"Let's have a look," said Grandad.

"Wait. Don't touch," said William. Grandad's hands had reached to feel the pipe, but they were now too big; they were too clumsy for the job.

Grandad leaned on the slopstone and watched William.

"That's a Macclesfield dandy. I've seen me Grandfather smoke one many a time. But I've never seen one not broken sooner or later. It must be his—and in the garden—all this while, and not hurt."

The last of the soil was out of the bowl, and William unblocked the stem. He blew it clear. And then he sucked, breathed in. The air rasped through the stem.

William washed his hands. The soap was yellow, bone-shaped, sharp with earth. The grit stood out.

Grandad put four potatoes in the oven. "We'll get ourselves fettled while they're baking," he said.

He picked up a torch and went outside. At the end of the house there was a low room built on. Grandad kept rubbish in it. The house was old, and nothing was ever thrown away, because, with so much rubbish over so many years, some of it was always useful.

A jumble of iron and wood lay in a corner. It was the remains of a loom. William could remember when it stood upright and he used to play on it. But all the softwood was worm-eaten, and one day it had collapsed under him.

The iron was newly bright from a saw. It was the iron that Grandad had curved in the swage block to the bellows handle.

"Catch hold on these," Grandad pulled some rags out of a drawer and gave them to William. They were soft and slippery. When he squeezed them, they crumpled up small, but sprang open as soon as he let go.

Grandad dismantled what was left of the loom, choosing only the good oak. The rest he smashed to kindling with his boot. "I've been meaning to rimson this glory hole for years," he said. "It's got you can't move, there's that much clutter."

Grandad and William carried the oak into the house. Grandad brewed the tea, and searched out an empty tobacco tin.

"Put Grandfather's pipe in that," he said, "and pack it round with them rags against it getting broken."

"What must I do with it?" said William.

"Keep it," said Grandad. "You found it; I

43

didn't. But let it lay there, so as I can see at it a while."

He opened the oven door and pulled out the potatoes, and he sat with William, and they ate them with salt and drank the tea. The potatoes were burnt black on one side and raw the other. Grandad kept looking at the pipe and shaking his head. He was laughing.

"And it was in the tater hogg?" he said.

"Must've been," said William.

"It figures," said Grandad.

"How?" said William.

"He was a rum un," said Grandad. "What you might call a Sunday saint and a Monday devil. It was his music, you see. Oh, he was the only best ringer and singer for miles, and he played every instrument he could lay hand to. Sunday at Chapel, regular. But Monday, and he was down your throat before you could open your mouth. Nothing vindictive, though. And I never did hear him swear. Not that he

couldn't. What! He knew the words, right enough. He could've sworn tremendous. He could've sworn the cross off an ass's back. But he never did. He never had to. His mind was that quick. And he did love to argue. Choose what you said, he'd put the other side, even when he agreed with you. And another thing—there wasn't one could take his drink as well as that old youth; there wasn't!"

Grandad pushed the dishes aside and opened his toolbox. William covered the pipe, closed the lid and put the tin in his pocket, by the key. Grandad set the two lengths of split-ash handle on the table and laid the bent iron next to them. He stuck the poker in the fire and wedged it between the bars of the grate. Then he sorted through the loom wood, made a stack of pieces, and marked them off all the same length with a foot rule and a pencil.

When all was tidy, he began to work.

He used the table as a bench, and cut the

marked oak on the line with a tenon saw. He started each cut by drawing the saw backwards, towards him, three times. Then he was away, cutting true, his hand and thumb clamped to the wood and the table.

"He used to go busking for beer, round and about!" Grandad laughed again. "Him and old Bob Sumner, Joe Swindells and Tom Wood. They were the Hough Band, of a Sunday, playing hymns. But the rest of the week they called theirselves the Hough Fizzers. And didn't they pop!"

He had cut the oak into eighteen-inch lengths. He fixed the two halves of ash that distance apart, and parallel, and nailed a length of oak across at the bottom of the curve of the handle. Behind it he put another; and so he went on. He worked without waste, and easily. The nails went into the oak and ash without bending.

"Well, one night, they'd had a right good night round the farms, and they were on their way back from The Bull's Head at

Mottram, very fresh, and they come to a quickthorn hedge, and the other side of it was a potato hogg as belonged to Jesse Leah.

"Now old Jesse, he'd stuck a two-three pieces of stove pipe through the top, with a little cowl on it, to ventilate the middle of the hogg, you see.

"Well, just then, up comes the moon behind the hogg and the bit of stove pipe, and Grandfather, he says, 'Wait on,' he says. 'Some there are going to bed. Let's give them a tune!' And they serenaded that potato hogg till morning. But Grandmother! Didn't she give him some stick, at after!"

Grandad turned the whole frame over, picked up the two strips of iron, and fitted them. He took a screw, held it in one of the countersunk holes, and drove it home. Now, for the first time, Grandad could be seen to be working. He grunted and sweated, and didn't talk. His grip on the screwdriver made his spark-pocked hand white, and once a screw started to bite, he kept it turning without rest until its head was flush with the iron.

But when he stood back, there was a sledge.

He sawed off the ends of the bellows handle that was now two runners level with the end of the iron that shod them.

Grandad left the sledge and came to sit in his chair by the fire. He rubbed his forehead.

"You mustn't let them screws stop turning," he said, "else they'll stick for evermore, and you'll not shift them. They'll shear, first."

He examined the poker. "Keep him that color," he said. He opened the corner cupboard above his chair. It was full of string and rope. He chose a length of rope, sash cord, like the sash cord that held the counterweight of the yard door above the cellar.

Grandad spat on the poker, tested its whiteness with his thumb, pressed it against the upcurve of one of the runners. The wood hissed and smoked, and the poker sank through. When it cooled, Grandad reheated it and pressed again. The room was full of the sweet smell of ash. There was a hole in the curve, like a black-rimmed eye.

Grandad burned through the other runner, threaded the cord into both eyes, knotted the ends, and the sledge was complete.

"Is that for me?" said William, not daring to.

"Well, it's not for me!" said Grandad.

"For me own? For me very liggy own?"

"Ay. Get that up Lizzie Leah's and see what Allmans have to say. Loom and forge."

Grandad threw the scrap wood on the coals. It sent flames of every color into the chimney. "They'll take no harm," said

Grandad. "It's sparks you must watch. Once they set in the thatch, the whole roof can fly on fire."

William leaned over the hearth to look up the chimney. The sparks spiraled and died in the blackness. But there was something bright, reflecting flame.

"Grandad?"

"Ay?"

"There's two horseshoes hanging in the chimney."

"I know there is," said Grandad.

"But they're clean. There's no soot on them."

"I know there isn't."

William reached into the chimney with his hand.

"Leave them," said Grandad. "They're not for you. Not yet."

"What are they?"

"Me and your Grandma's wedding."

"Up the chimney?" said William.

"Of course they're up the chimney," said

Grandad. "Of course they're clean. I put them there forty-two years ago, and I clean them of a Sunday. What are you staring like a throttled earwig for?"

"I didn't know," said William.

"You didn't know?" said Grandad. "A high-learned youth like you didn't know? Your Grandma and me, we'd have let every stick of furniture go first, and the house, before we'd have parted from them. They're our wedding. They're your father and your uncles. They're you. Do you not see? They're us!

"Your friends and your neighbors give them to the wedding. No one says. It happens. And it happens as the smith's at his forge one night, and happens to find the money by the door. And he makes the shoes alone, swage block and anvil; and we put them in the chimneypiece. Mind you, I'd know Tommy Latham's work anywhere. But we don't let on. It's all a mystery. Now get up them fields."

There were voices in the road. William put on his balaclava and mittens.

Grandad lifted the sledge down. "She'll stick a toucher at first," he said, "while the iron finds a polish. But then she'll go, with that bevel to her. And at after, all she'll want is a spot of oil, against rust in summer.

"I feel the wind's bristled up," he said. "I'll not come out."

William went down the path from the house; Grandad closed the blackout behind him.

The sledge jerked a little at first, and left stains that showed in the moonlight, but the curved, strong iron, countersunk screwed, rode on the frost better than the tin runners of the broken crate had done. The swage block down in the cellar worked on the hill.

Lizzie Leah's was crowded. People were coming from both directions along the road. William pulled the sledge up the bottom field. It was heavy, but the rope didn't cut, and it was all strong and in balance and carried a lot of its own weight.

There were more of the bigger boys at night, and they racketed over the hump. William had to dodge through the gateway between runs. There was the flurried rattle of approach, the gasp in the air, and the beat of the landing. William set himself above the hump; but before he could start, a sledge came at him from above, veered to the barbed wire, and the rider skidded off, over the hump and through the gate.

It was Stewart Allman.

They were coming in twos and threes and even in packs, starting together and racing for the gate.

Stewart Allman whistled through his fingers. "Wait on!" he shouted up the hill. "We've a betty!"

William sat on the sledge, looked over his shoulder, but there was no one coming, so he heeled himself forward.

The sledge moved gently, surely, sensitive to touch. He could steer it, and just as he had felt the road and the bicycle through the slow movement of Grandad's coat, he felt the hill through the sledge, as if he flowed over it, never left it. There were no jolts. The sledge crushed ruts and ran only on the true hill.

"Where've you got that from?" said Stewart Allman.

"Me Grandad," said William. "He made it."

"Let's have a go," said Stewart Allman.

They were walking back. The axle grease on William's clogs let no snow gather. Now Stewart Allman was trying to keep up.

"Barley mey fog shot no back bargains," said William.

"I only want a go—just one."

"You pull it, then," said William, and gave the rope to Stewart Allman.

"Eh! What's it made of?"

"Oak, mostly," said William.

"It weighs a ton," said Stewart Allman.

He was out of breath when they reached the middle of the top field.

He lay on the sledge, with the rope tucked under him, and gripped the runners where they curled up at the end of the forge-bellows handle. The sledge was longer than he was.

"Give us a shove."

But the sledge began to move as soon as Stewart Allman lifted his feet. It didn't snatch or creak or waver. It moved straight down and across the hill, and so marvelously that it was only when the other sledgers, climbing back, stopped to watch it pass them that William realized how fast it was going.

Stewart Allman made no noise. The sledge hit the hump and reared and stood on end. William heard the runners twang the barbed wire, and the sledge and Stewart Allman disappeared.

William jumped down the field sideways,

using his clog irons to grip. He found the sledge. It had snapped the wire. Stewart Allman was in a snow drift.

William grabbed the sledge. "You're not safe!" he yelled. "You might've bust this one, too, you daft beggar!"

He ran up the hill, pulling the undamaged sledge. He staggered and ran, angry, unthinking. But he had to stop when he came to the corner post of the top of the field—the top of the top field, where nobody went.

William turned the sledge against the hill, and sat down.

He watched the others. They couldn't see him by the stump. He watched moon and starlight and shapes gliding. Another cloud was coming from the north, but it was a long way off.

The air-raid sirens sounded the alert, village after village, spreading like bonfires. He settled down to watch.

As soon as the bombers were heard, the

searchlights would be switched on and the guns would start to fire. They were in Johnny Baguley's field, less than a mile away.

"Eh! You! Public Enemy Number One! We're waiting!"

It was Stewart Allman.

William looked down. The next highest sledge was a long way below him. He could crawl under the fence and down the other side of the hill, but Stewart Allman would know. William would be ambushed.

The field was waiting. Dark patches looking at him.

He stood up and tugged the sledge round. As soon as it was in line with the slope, it began to move. He shortened the rope.

William sat astride, his heels braced. He let out the rope, lay back, and eased the pressure off his heels. He felt the sledge start, and then he felt no speed, only a rhythm of the hill. The sledge found its own course; a touch corrected it. As he went faster, William used his clogs for balance. The steering moved into his hands and arms, then his shoulders, and then he was going so fast and so true that he could steer with a turn of his head.

The watching groups were a flicker as he passed, and his speed grew on the more trampled snow.

He saw the hump and the gate, but saw nothing to fear. He took in more rope, gripped, and the forge-bellows runners breasted the air without shock. He pulled on the rope and kiltered his head to the right. His weight had brought him forward, and the curved runners were at his shoulder. Then the trailing corners of the loom iron took the weight, the front of the sledge dropped away, and William was lying back again, coasting along the bottom field.

He put down his heels and stopped at the hedge.

Stewart Allman arrived.

"Any bones broken?" he said.

"No," said William.

"We thought you'd be killed."

"Get off with you!" said William. "It's dead safe. Me Grandad made it."

"Will you go again?" said Stewart Allman. "From the top."

"It's a heck of a climb," said William.

"I'll give you a pull to half way," said Stewart Allman.

"What about your sledge?"

"It's no weight. Honest. Will you?"

"OK."

Stewart Allman took both sledges and floundered up the field. William dusted off the snow powder that had sprayed over him in a plume.

"He's going again!" said Stewart Allman when they reached the others. "Stand back!"

He handed over the rope to William, and William went on alone.

"I was going to, anyway," he said when he was at the top.

He set off. It had not been imagined. He was not alone on a sledge. There was a line, and he could feel it. It was a line through hand and eye, block, forge and loom to the hill. He owned them all; and they owned him.

"Good-lad-Dick," said Stewart Allman after the second run, but he didn't offer to pull the sledge, and the others had lost interest. William shouted whenever he was ready to go from the top, and the way was left clear; but that was all.

The Dorniers came in from the east, and the Heinkels flew overhead. The search-lights swiveled around the sky, but never saw anything, and the guns began to fire. William watched from the top of the field.

A battery of guns opened up, the flash and then the noise. Everybody stopped sledging when the shrapnel began to fall. It was easier to find on Lizzie Leah's than it was in the village. The fragments zipped and fizzed into the snow. William collected until his pockets were full. He needn't have swapped his incendiary. He had more shrapnel than he could keep.

The others soon began sledging again.

They were having pack races to the gate. If everybody arrived at the same time, it was a calamity. If someone got there first but lost control, he had to escape from his own crash before he was hit by the rest.

William pushed off from the top when he heard Stewart Allman shout, "On your marks!" At "Get set!" he was lying back. By "Go!" he was coming down at thirty miles an hour, the spray from his heels hitting his face like freezing sand. He curved round the pack on a new course, and cut in to beat them to the hump. The moment in the air was worth any climb.

He found he could leave at "Get set!" and still have the freedom of the gate. To wait until "Go!" was dangerous.

William was holding on his heels for the next run when he saw how like bombers the pack were in their tight group. He started off. They had opened formation by the time he reached them.

He came in on the bombers from above and out of the sun. Two crossed his sights, and he gave them a burst. They went down together. Another tried to dodge him, and crashed. He raced through the pack and settled on the leader's tail. The leader climbed hard at the hump, but William caught his fusilage with a runner, and the leader spun out of control and hit the tree.

William landed. The leader was struggling in a thorn hedge. "You're flaming crackers, you are!" said Stewart Allman. "Look what you've done!"

The field really was littered. The sledge had sent the pack careering all ends up.

"I didn't mean to," said William. "I was a Spitfire."

"He was only being a Spitfire!" Stewart

64

Allman shouted. He limped over to the dump and dropped his broken sledge. "And I've got a sprained Heinkel."

"I didn't mean it," said William.

"Come on, you daft oddment," said Stewart Allman. "We were packing in now, any road. That shrapnel's brogged the snow. It's busting the sledges."

"Mine's all right," said William.

"Well, ours aren't," said Stewart Allman. "But play again tomorrow, when it's snowed."

"Play again," said William. "I told you that black cloud was snow."

"It wasn't," said Stewart Allman.

"It was!"

"It wasn't."

"It snowed a blizzard!" said William.

"Yes, but that wasn't the cloud."

"Where did the blizzard come from, then?"

"Out of the sky," said Stewart Allman. "The white bits."

"But the cloud went at the same time as the blizzard," said William.

"That's why," said Stewart Allman. "There was a wind in the cloud, and it blew the snow away. Now there's a proper snow cloud for you."

He pointed to the north. The moon shone on billows, reflecting light. "See, clever clogs?"

"Play again," said William.

"Play again."

William set off for home. The guns were still firing. Stewart Allman had been right. It was going to snow.

He came to Grandad's house. There was a bicycle propped against the wall. The air-raid warden often called for a cup of tea if it wasn't too late in the night.

The sledge runners had taken such a polish that the sledge kept banging William's ankles; so when he stopped, he had to swing the rope past him in an arc.

There was more than one bicycle. There

were several, against the wall under the thatch. William pulled the sledge up the path and lodged it by the door. He opened the door, went in and closed it, and drew the blackout curtain aside.

The room was empty, but the lamp was lit. There were too many unexpected smells: facepowder, whisky, cigarette smoke. But the room was empty. William listened. He felt and heard the house heavy above him. Nobody was talking, but there was a weight in the room overhead.

Lamplight and shadow were on the bent stairs. William climbed up until he could see.

The bedroom was thatched rafters down to the floor, and it was full of people, still wearing their coats, and standing, pressed by the roof, around Grandad's bed.

William worked between the gathered legs towards the bed.

Voices were whispering, and he was sure he knew the people, but now they were figures darkening him.

He moved a coat hem, and looked straight into Grandad's eyes. The blue eyes and the sharp nose. There was such a clearness in the eyes that William felt that they were speaking to him. Of all the people crowded there, Grandad looked only at William. He must be speaking to him.

"Grandad."

The eyes answered with their fierce blue.

"Grandad, I've been up Lizzie Leah's, and it's a belter. The irons have got a right polish on them now." Someone turned against William as he was kneeling. Grandad sighed, or spoke. "What, Grandad?"

The fierce, kind eyes were still urgent, but that small movement had taken William out of their sight. They were looking at what was before them, at nothing more.

William pushed away from the bed. The coats fell like a curtain. He went backwards to the stairs, and down.

It was a big room. He had never known it empty. William stood in the room and listened to the weight in the house upended. All in the bedroom, no one below. The table cleared, but with sawdust in the cracks.

William stood at the chimney. He saw the corner cupboard, the chair.

He spilled the shrapnel across the floor, and when he was rid of it and had only the key in the pocket, the pipe in the tin, he reached into the darkness, and closed his hands.

"Tom Fobble's Day!"

William held the two gleaming horseshoes.

"No back bargains!"

He ran from the house. The horseshoes pulled his jacket out of shape, but their weight was light as he ran with his sledge to the top of Lizzie Leah's.

The line did hold. Through hand and eye, block, forge and loom to the hill and

all that he owned, he sledged sledged sledged for the black and glittering night and the sky flying on fire and the expectation of snow.